CHILDREN WHO COMMITTED MURDERS

By. Wilhelm Lang

ISBN: 9798651764952

Published by VAX Books

Cover design by VAX Graphix

VaxbookZ.com

This is a true crime list about 10 children who committed murders.

DISCLAIMER AND WARNING: Some of the contents are graphic and very disturbing, especially because many of the victims were children themselves. Reader discretion is advised.

Table of contents

INTRODUCTION

It's rare for a child to commit a serious crime , and even rarer for that act to be murder.
So when these cases make the news, they fascinate readers, and stay in the public consciousness long after the trials have ended.

Murder is such an extreme crime that even what motivates adult killers can remain mysterious. Getting to the bottom of what pushed a child to kill is even more difficult.

Many such crimes involve children attacking those younger than them, usually with an age gap of six to eight years.

Needing to feel powerful comes into some of the cases, as does curiosity - wanting to know what killing feels like.

Below, we take a closer look at 10 of the most chilling child murderers:

1-Mary Bell

Mary Flora Bell was 11 when, in 1968, was convicted for the murder of two little boys in Scotswood, Newcastle upon Tyne, England, and many believe that she wouldn't have stopped killing if she wasn't arrested.

On May 1968 the dead body of 4-year-old **Martin Brown** was found on the floor of a derelict house by a group of boys that were playing in the area. Blood and saliva were trickling down the side of his cheek. The boys reported that almost immediately after their discovery, they saw Mary Bell and her 13-year-old friend **Norma Bell** (same surname, no relation) coming toward the house and stopping right by the window next to Martin's body.

Upon investigating, police found no evidence of foul play and believed, since there was an empty bottle of aspirin nearby, that the death was accidental. The official report declared the cause of death "open".

It wasn't until another little boy's dead body was found weeks later, that they started to look at Martin's death as a homicide.

In July, 3-year-old **Brian Howe** was strangled to death, his body abandoned in an industrial area of the town, mutilated on the thighs and genitals with a pair of scissors that laid in the nearby grass, the letter "M" carved with a razor on his belly. Inspector James Dobson, who investigated on the case, stated that there was a "terrible playfulness" about these mutilations.

Mary and Norma immediately stood out as suspicious to the investigators, both because they have been behaving strangely with Martin Brown's family, inappropriately keep asking questions about him with a creepy grin on their faces, and because they were literally showing excitement about Brian Howe's death.

When questioned by police, Mary admitted that she and Norma had seen Brian on the day he died, claiming that she saw a specific 8-year-old boy hitting Brian and, afterwards, playing with a pair of scissors. Her testimony was considered unreliable, though, as the boy in question had a strong alibi and no details about the scissors had been disclosed to the public. By mentioning the scissors, she implicated herself. The two girls were questioned again after Brian's funeral in August and Norma accused Mary of having strangled Brian and bringing her to see his body. Mary responded that this was a lie and made an official statement saying that she was incapable of harming anything or anyone and blaming Norma.

Both girls were arrested for the murder of Brian Howe and incarcerated at the Newcastle West End police station.

Their trial started on December 5 at the Newcastle Assizes Moothall and lasted for 9 days.

The prosecution suggested that whoever killed Brian Howe also killed Martin Brown, recounting about the suspicious behaviour of the girls, of Mary's long history of violence towards other children (Norma's little sister included) and of how they vandalized their school overnight leaving behind scribbled notes such as "I murder so THAT I may come back" and "we did murder Martain brown Fuckof you Bastard".

While Norma reacted childishly and was considered a mere victim of Mary's manipulations, the latter was the centre of press attention. Everyone in the courtroom reportedly were "watching her with a horrified kind of curiosity", especially because she showed no emotions whatsoever and, on the contrary, her mother, Betty Bell, didn't do nothing but put on a show of dramatic wailing and sobbing.

Psychologists and psychiatrists that examined Mary Bell over the years stated that she exhibited the classic symptoms of psychopathology, seen the lack of remorse for her actions and her completely unemotional behaviour. Dr. Westbury stated: "Manipulation of people is her primary aim" and all those who met her concurred that she was very intelligent. She clearly had issues with bonding with others due to her family background.

Her mother, Betty, was well-known for being a prostitute, she gave birth to Mary at the age of 17. Her biological father's identity is still a mystery, but Mary was raised by her stepfather Billy Bell, who also had quite a reputation in town. Baby Mary was often neglected by Betty: she tried to abandon her, sell her and even allegedly kill her numerous times – mostly with drugs - but always eventually kept her just to gain sympathy from others. Mary accused her mother to have used her during her prostitution, forcing her to engage in sexual acts with her clients.

Although this abuse would explain Mary's disturbed behaviour, all her accusations remain alleged.

The jury found Mary guilty of manslaughter in both Brian Howe's and Martin Brown's deaths, even if neither she nor Norma ever admitted their responsibility for the latter. The judge pronounced a sentence of "Detention for Life" for an indeterminate amount of time, in hope that she could reform. All that was given to Norma was a 3 year probation for breaking in the school.

Mary was incarcerated at the Red Bank Special School in Lancashire, a high security all-boys facility, until 1973. During her stay there she seemed reformed at first, but growing up she started to have issues, as she started to sexually provoke the boys and to wound herself with cuts. She was then moved to a prison for women where she convinced herself to be gay and even asked for a sex change, because "it was the idea of not being me", she claimed. In 1977 she escaped from a less secured facility and was moved to a hostel a few months before her release in 1980, at the age of 23.

After this time, Mary Bell allegedly became a complete different person. The court granted her to change her name to protect her identity, she got married and had a daughter, whose birth, she claims, gave her a new awareness of her crimes.

Although she collaborated with author Gitta Sereny in writing the second of her biographies "**Cries Unheard: the Story of Mary Bell**", published in 1998, she never admitted her crimes and changed versions of the events many times, still implicating Norma in having responsibility in Brian Howe's death and portraying her mother Betty as the main villain of her story.

2-Joshua Phillips

The case of **Maddie Clifton**'s murder at the hands of young Joshua Phillips in Jacksonville, Florida, made a lot of news in the late '90s, not only because of its gruesomeness and Phillips's obvious guilt, but also because the sentence is still controversial under the American constitutional point of view.

8-year-old Maddie Clifton disappeared on November 8, 1998. She failed to return home for dinner after spending an evening out to play. Her mother Sheila reported her missing to 911 and that night the family and the neighbours searched for her with flashlights.

Police and hundreds of volunteers kept looking for Maddie over the next 7 days. A big reward was offered, flyers were distributed around town, even the FBI became involved... until Melissa Phillips, a neighbour of the Clifton family, made a terrible discovery.

On the morning of the seventh day after Maddie's disappearance, she went to her 14-year-old son Joshua's bedroom to clean up. She noticed some water leaking on the floor at the end of the waterbed, accompanied by a strange smell. She pulled apart the baseboard to check under the bed and saw a human foot. She immediately ran outside to call a police officer and led him to Joshua's bedroom.

Maddie Clifton's rotting body had been hidden inside the pedestal of Joshua Phillips's waterbed the whole time. She was beaten over the head and stabbed at least nine times in the chest and twice in the neck, undressed from the waist down.

The boy was arrested at his school and when was questioned by police, he confessed to the murder.

According to him, Maddie, who not only was his neighbour, but also his friend and playmate, came over to his house on the early evening of the day she disappeared, asking him to play baseball together. She was a tomboy and loved playing that game. At first, Joshua said no, because his father would be getting home soon and would be angry if she was there, but he later agreed. The two of them played together in his backyard, until a ball that Joshua hit with his baseball bat hit hard Maddie on her head. Since the girl started to scream in pain, Joshua panicked and carried her to his bedroom. Maddie's moaning and screams became so loud that he started to hit her on the head with his baseball bat and stab her in the throat with a pocketknife numerous times in order to silence her. Then he finally proceeded to shove her, still alive, under his bed and went to wash up.

He claimed that he panicked because scared of getting in trouble, that his father, Steve Phillips, who severely forbade anyone in their house when he and his wife were absent, would have punished him. As a psychologist hired by the family attorney confirmed, Joshua was terrified of his father. He said that if he did something wrong "[his father] always had kind of short temper", that he "sometimes never knew what he'd do".

Joshua was taken into custody and his trial began on July 1999. It had to be moved from Jacksonville to Bartow, Florida, because of its intense news coverage. It only lasted 2 days because Joshua's lawyer, Richard Nichols, presented no witnesses or evidence. The entire defence was a closing argument. The only defence he could argue was that the murder wasn't premeditated, his family members talked about how he was a good boy who has never shown a hint of violence before (the Cliftons and his teachers have had the same impression) and how sorry he was for killing Maddie, for which he still has no explanation. "Maybe I should get some kind of counselling or something to find out what's wrong with me" he later said during an interview.

The testimony of a neurologist finding that Joshua had "bilateral frontal lobe lesions", which can impair judgment as well as cause panic, wasn't allowed by the judge as evidence to be presented to court. This theory was also shared by Joshua's mother.

On the other hand, the prosecutor Harry Shorstein suggested that the murder may have been sexually motivated, as Joshua had previously talked to Maddie about sex and that was looking at violent pornographic websites in the half hour preceding the murder, which could have trigged his violence. This would also explain why Maddie's body was nude from her waist down (although autopsy found no evidence of sexual assault), but neither this evidence was admitted to the trial.

In his closing argument, the defence attorney Nichols urged jurors to convict Joshua of manslaughter and filed a motion to sentence him as juvenile. After deliberating for 2 hours, the jury convicted Joshua of first-degree murder and Judge Charles Arnold sentenced him to life in prison with no possibility of parole.

Joshua's life in prison is going well, in spite of his remorse for his terrible actions. He graduated with a paralegal degree in 2007 and now works as a law clerk advising fellow inmates. "I don't know if I deserve a second chance or not" he said, "but I know I want the chance".

His no-parole life sentence was later up to discussion, as in 2012 the US Supreme Court ruled that sentencing juveniles to mandatory life without parole is unconstitutional. As a result of retroactive application of this ruling, in September 2016, Joshua's attorney appealed to the court and he was granted a new sentencing hearing in August 2017.

The sentence arrived on November 17th, 2017, which resulted in Judge Waddell Wallace warranting life in prison for Joshua. "I believe this is one of the most rare and unusual crimes that warrants life in prison" he wrote, because "[Joshua's] actions were motivated by deviant, prurient intentions" that "represent a level of depravity that cannot be explained or attributed to immaturity, impetuosity or recklessness or headless risk taking".

This was a satisfying sentence for the Clifton family, but Joshua's mother stated that an appeal with be filed. The case is up for an automatic review in about six years.

3- Graham Young

Although most of Graham Young's homicides occurred in adulthood, his disturbed mind pushed him to start killing, or trying to kill, at the young age of 14. Hadn't he been released from his first conviction, the following victims would have lived.

Molly Young was a 37-year-old housewife living in St. Albans, Hertfordshire, England, with her husband Fred Young and his children from a previous marriage, Winifred and Graham, when she died on Easter Saturday of 1962 after months of suffering painful symptoms such as vomiting, diarrhea, excruciating stomach pain, loss of hair and weight. It was concluded that her death was due to the prolapse of a bone at the top of her spinal column, an injury connected to a blow to the head when she was involved in a bus crash. Upon suggestion of her 14-year-old stepson, Molly was cremated. In his father and sister's eyes, young Graham had something to do with all of this in the first place.

Graham's biological mother, Bessie, tragically died of tuberculosis only three months after his birth in 1947 and he was raised for the following two years by his aunt and uncle, while his elder sister went to live with their grandparents. Their father remarried in 1950, to Molly, and reunited the family. The separation from his aunt's household, though, caused little Graham a big distress.

He went on to become a solitary child obsessed with nonfiction books about murders, insanely fascinated with Adolf Hitler, the occult and, above all things, poisons. His schoolmates kept their distance from Graham, finding him creepy and dubbing him "The Mad Professor". Some of them told of how he would try to get them to sniff ether with him, and also - claiming to be a part of a local coven - engage them in occult ceremonies, which had involved cat sacrifices in at least one occasion. He used to spend long hours in the library reading books of chemistry, poisons and forensic science, eventually gaining the expertise of a chemistry post-graduate.

Knowing about his son's "hobby", his father bought Graham a chemistry set as a reward for his high school grades. That's when the boy's thirst of toxicological knowledge started to grow insatiable and lethal.

Armed with the fake ID of "M.E. Evans", aged 13, he managed to convince two separate local chemists that he was 17 and obtained "for study purposes" enough antimony, arsenic, digitalis and thallium to kill 300 people.

In order to test his knowledge of poisons, he began his experiments on fellow science enthusiast and only friend Christopher Williams. The two kids often spent lunchtime together at school, so it would be easy for Graham to inject harmful substances in Christopher's meals. He suffered an extended period of vomiting, painful cramps and headaches. Doctors couldn't diagnose his illness, just suggested that the symptoms were those of a severe migraine.

Christopher was lucky to survive, as Graham decided that he and other school friends didn't satisfy his scientific curiosity anymore. He needed to keep tabs on the symptoms, so he started to focus on someone he could observe at closer quarters... his own family.

In November 1961, Graham served a cup of tea to his sister Winifred, but she found it so bitter that she threw it away. Later that day, she felt sick on the train to work and was rushed to the hospital. Doctors concluded that she had been poisoned with belladonna.

Fred Young, even if doubtful, just thought that his son had inadvertently contaminated the food and did nothing but warn him to be more careful. It didn't take long until his wife Molly became ill, more and more, until, in that fatal Easter Saturday, he found her writhed in agony in the back garden while Graham was staring out of the kitchen window in fascination. He had been poisoning his stepmother with antimony for months, but when he understood that her organism had developed a tolerance to it, he gave her enough thallium to kill six people, murdering her.

He kept on poisoning his family members, his father included, who suspected his guilt but still didn't take any action.

It was Graham's school chemistry teacher, Geoffrey Hughes, the one who reported him to police after, upon searching the boy's school desk, he found bottles of poisons, drawings of dying men and essays about famous murders.

Thinking it was for a job, Graham was interviewed by a police psychiatric in disguise who, in order to ascertain his mental state, persuaded the boy to talk about his expertise with poisons and later reported his horrified findings to the authorities.

At first, when he was arrested in May 1962, Graham denied his guilt, but later broke down and admitted to have poisoned his father, sister and friend Christopher Williams. "It grew on me like drug habit" he said, "except it was not me who was taking the drugs". No charges were brought against him for Molly's death, since it was impossible to get useful evidence from her ashes.

At the age of 14, he was convicted for the poisonings and sent to Broadmoor maximum security hospital with the order that he was not to be released without the permission of the Home Secretary for 15 years, but, upon a psychiatric recommendation, stayed only 8 years.

His thirst wasn't satisfied at all and he became a serial killer known as "The Teacup Poisoner".

Graham was suspected for the death of a fellow prisoner named John Berridge of cyanide poisoning, but since there were no cyanide anywhere in the prison, the official verdict was that the man had taken his own life. He tried to poison the staff by putting bleach in the coffee and probably planned to poison nearly a hundred of people with a cleanser that was found in the communal tea urn. Afterwards, he became a model prisoner, which misled the prison psychiatrist into thinking that he was "no longer obsessed with poisons, violence and mischief" and let him out on February 1971, aged 23.

In the following months he poisoned numerous people among roommates and co-workers, killing two: Bob Egle, 59 years old, and Fred Biggs, 60 years old. Both of them suffered savagely and met gruesome deaths. Graham had served them tea with thallium, a substance used in their workplace, a photographic supply firm in Bovingdon, Hertfordshire, and kept a diary where he recorded daily every symptom each of his victims suffered. This would be the biggest evidence that led him to downfall.

Following the suspicions the firm doctor had on him after a discussion they had together about thallium poisoning, he was arrested in November that same year and his trial took place on June 1972. A reporter stated that Graham "came across as incredibly creepy", that he "just had this unnerving aura about him".

"For him the whole thing was one big chemistry experiment" said his defence attorney, Peter Goodman.

Although the young man was confident that there wasn't enough evidence to prove beyond doubt that only he could have administered the poisons, so much that he confessed his guilt to the police only to deny it on court, he was finally convicted of two murders, two attempted murders and two counts of administering poison and sentenced to life in prison.

He served his sentence in the maximum security Parkhurst prison on the Isle of Wight, a place reserved for Britain's most dangerous prisoners. There, he met and befriended fellow inmate Ian Brady, one of the "Moors Murderers" pair, bonding over their shared fascination with Nazi Germany. Brady developed a one sided infatuation towards Graham, asserting in his biography that "power and death were his aphrodisiacs".

When asked if he felt remorse, Graham replied "No, that would be hypocritical. What I feel is the emptiness of my soul" and his wish of fame and immortality was granted when a waxwork made of him was installed in the "Chamber of Horrors" in Madam Tussaud's Museum in London, alongside Dr. Crippen's, one of his heroes.

Graham died in 1990, aged 42, of heart attack. This was the official diagnosis, but some suspected that he killed himself in a final act of power.

Considering the outrageous circumstances of Graham's case, UK laws were tightened on monitoring mentally ill offenders after release.

4- Jon Venables + Robert Thompson

A pair of troubled but not considered delinquents 10-year-olds abducted, tortured and ruthlessly killed a toddler in 1993 Liverpool, becoming the youngest convicted murderers of the 20th century.

In the early afternoon of Friday February 12, 1993, young mother Denise Bulger decided to accompany her brother's girlfriend Nicola to shop at the New Strand Shopping Centre in Bootle, Merseyside, England, bringing her almost 3-year-old son **James**, as she always did. That day, James was full of energy and his mother tried her best to keep him quiet despite of his efforts to get free and play around. Until they reached their final stop of their shopping day: the butcher's shop. She got distracted just for a minute while paying the butcher and James was gone. Denise panicked and went to the security office seeking help to find her son, whose name and description were announced over the loudspeakers... all in vain. She called the police and the search for James Bulger began..

James's disappearance made the evening news and after one report that he was spotted by the Liverpool canal, investigators planned to drag its waters, meanwhile authorities watched the security videos taken at the shopping centre, hoping to catch a glimpse of James's abductor. They found what they were looking for, but they realized with disbelief that they were not dealing with an adult. The low-resolution CCTV footage showed two young boys taking James by the hand and leading him out of the shopping centre at 3:42 pm. Hoping that someone would recognize them, the police released the video stills of the boys to the media to be shown on television and in the papers. More searches were organized both in the canal and on land for the following two days, until the gruesome discovery.

Four boys who went up to the Walton railroad to look for footballs on Sunday afternoon found on the tracks what at first they thought was a cat, then a doll, torn into two by the train. It was James's corpse. He had been laid by the waist onto the rail, with his upper body on the inside of the tracks, hidden within the coat. The lower half, completely undressed, had been carried further down the tracks. James had been severely tortured and beaten around the head and possibly sexually assaulted, since investigators suspected that some AA batteries found close to the body were inserted into his anus and the pathologist later reported that his foreskin had been forcibly retracted. On one cheek, a patterned bruise appeared, which indicated the imprint from a shoe. The toddler suffered so many injuries that none could be isolated as the fatal blow. It was concluded that he was still alive when left on the tracks, but already dead when the train hit him. More evidence found nearby the crime scene included a tin of blue paint, a heavy iron bar with bloodstains on it, bricks and stones, also covered in blood.

The police held press conferences showing some of the evidence to find witnesses and checked Friday's absentee lists from schools, convinced that the two young abductors captured on the

CCTV cameras were teenagers. Many parents called the station to report their own kids as suspects until police received a call from an anonymous woman, reporting that her neighbour's son, who resembled one of the boys in the video, had blue paint on his jacket sleeve and had skipped school on Friday with his friend.

These two suspects from Merseyside, who were brought in for questioning, were Jon Venables and Robert Thompson, both aged 10.

Jon, the second of three children, had been showing signs of anti-social behaviour for years, morbidly seeking the attention of his parents, who were too focused on his siblings as they both required special care due to developmental problems. At school he was hyper and easily distracted, victim of bullies because of his predisposition for violent outbursts, and grew increasingly dangerous, first to himself, then to others, to the extent that he had to be transferred to another school. There he met Robert Thompson, with whom he felt tough and they became bullies not to feel outcasts anymore.

Robert, the fifth of six brothers, came from a much more disturbed family background. His father mercilessly beat his mother in front of their sons and she became violent and an alcoholic too, with the result that the boys were left to watch out for one other, even if truth was that they needed protection from one another. The oldest ones abused the youngest and almost all of them ended up having criminal records or attempting suicide at some point. The police and social workers knew the Thompson boys well.

Their teachers felt sympathy for Jon, since it was clear he was pleading for help, and described Robert as shy and quiet, yet manipulative of others and a liar. They noticed how they seemed to bring out the worst in each other and made efforts to keep them apart, although they had no control on them when they skipped school, which happened on regular basis.

Upon police questioning, it was proved that Jon and Robert were indeed playing truant for the nth time on that Friday February 12. They had decided to go the shopping centre to mess around and pocket whatever was in reach, like batteries, enamel paint, pens and pencils, a troll doll (which Robert collected), candy and other stuff. Until they got so bored that they decided to "get a kid", presumably Robert's idea. They planned to find a child to abduct, lead him to the busy road alongside the mall, and push him into the path of oncoming traffic. They tried to lure a two-year-old boy into following them at the TJ Hughes store, but were prevented by his mother. Then they spotted James Bulger by the butcher's shop door, Jon took him by the hand and within 2 minutes the three of them were outside the mall.

Jon, Robert and James wandered on busy roads from the Strand to Walton for a few hours. The two older boys sometimes protecting the little one from the traffic, sometimes kicking and punching him to have fun or to stop his cries for his mother. It was at the Liverpool canal that they first hurt James, picking him up and dropped him on his head. They were about to leave him there crying, but later decided to take him again. Many people noticed them, some even approached them asking if they needed help, but basically did nothing to rescue James, since everyone assumed they were older brothers walking around with their baby brother. These witnesses would later be called by the papers the "Liverpool 38" and shamed them for turning the other way.

They arrived at the Walton railway at approximately 5.30 pm. It was there that Jon and Robert started viciously attacking James. They flung the blue paint on his face into the left eye, threw stones at him, kicked him and beat him with bricks. They pulled off his shoes and pants, perhaps sexually assaulting him, and hit him with an iron bar. They finally laid his body, still alive, on the railroad tracks, hoping that the community would think it was an accident, and came back to their daily lives.

At first, when arrested and separately interviewed in the presence of their parents on Thursday February 18, Robert played the part of the tough one and denied his involvement in the murder, while Jon did nothing but cry and sink deep into remorse, finally admitting that he "did kill him". In spite of Jon's confession, investigators were sure that Robert participated somehow. The boy kept on insisting to blame Jon and lost it when he was asked if they removed James's pants and underwear and inserted the AA batteries into his rectum, starting to cry and saying "I'm not a pervert". Jon became hysterical as well because of that question.

On Saturday February 20, Jon Venables and Robert Thompson were charged with the abduction and murder of James Bulger and detained until their trial, which opened at Preston Crown Court on November 1, 1993, conducted as an adult trial. The judge ruled that the boys be known as Child A (Robert) and Child B (Jon).

While Jon won some sympathy with the court observers, since he seemed more contrite, anxious and "in thrall of Robert", this latter showed little emotion and was assumed to be the "guilty one". The both of them were indignant to listen as they accused each other of the murder when the court played the recorded police interviews. Especially Robert when he heard Jon claiming that he was like a girl because he played with dolls.

After the witnesses of Jon and Robert's teachers and the psychiatrists who examined them, the prosecution portrayed the two boys as equally liable, as they knew the severity of their crime. The evidence clearly indicated their guilt: the Strand security videos, blood-splattered bricks, stones, clothing, a tin of blue paint and a heavy bar; also, the imprint on James's cheek was conclusively linked to a bloody shoe belonging to Robert.

The defense countered that it was only a mischievous prank gone out of control, since they didn't intended to kill James at the time of the abduction or while walked him around Liverpool.

Jon and Robert were found guilty on Wednesday, November 24. The judge declared that the killing of James Bulger was "an act of unparalleled evil and barbarity", sentenced them to be detained "for very, very many years" and allowed the media to publish their names.

After the trial, Robert was held at the Barton Moss Secure Care Centre in Manchester and Jon was detained in a Red Bank secure unit in St. Helens on Merseyside (the same facility where Mary Bell was incarcerated 25 years before). The both of them received education and rehabilitation, even if they suffered post-traumatic stress disorder.

They were both released after serving their minimum tariff of eight years on February 2001, at the age of 19, were given new identities and moved to secret locations; also, an injunction prevented the media to publish details about them, because, as the Home Secretary stated, "there was a real and strong possibility that their lives would be at risk if their identities became known". The terms of their release included that they were not allowed to contact each other or the Bulger family.

While Robert is thought to have stuck to the terms of the license, Jon violated one and was returned to prison on March 7, 2010 to be charged with possession and distribution of child pornography images, after a number of more arrests for possession of cocaine. He was given a new identity and freed on parole on September 3, 2013.

For the second time since his release, Jon was put back in jail again after being caught with child porn, even using online dating websites in search of single mothers, in November 2017.

Reportedly, Jon is keeping on with his felonies because he feels untouchable. "He has had secret identities, costing ridiculous amounts of money and all at the cost of the taxpayer, and thinks he will continue to be protected" a source said. "And the sad thing is, he's probably correct".

On February 2018, a judge stated on court that Jon is a "continued high risk to children" and condemned him to a 40-month term sentence for possessing over 1.000 child abuse images and even a paedophile manual. He was moved to a new prison after fellow inmates discovered his identity and wanted to attack him.

James's mother Denise, who had always been sure that Jon would have re-offended, accused the probation service of 'covering up' for him and didn't accept Jon's apologise during this trial. As to James's father, Ralph, he told in an interview that he believes Jon could kill again, that "you can't rewire evil and that is what he is".

5- Jordan Brown

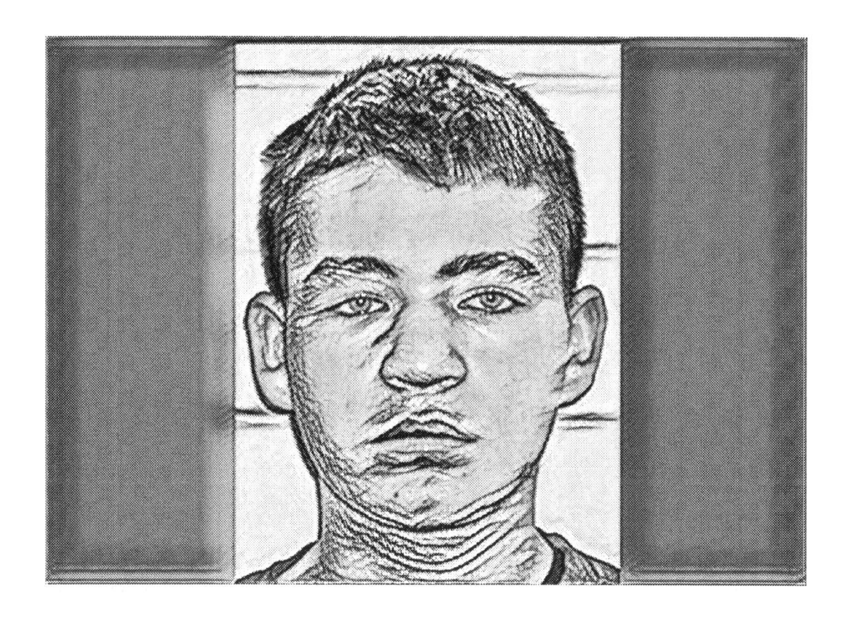

Jordan Brown's case reawakened the controversial issue of children being prosecuted as adults.

In the morning of February 20, 2009, **Kenzie Marie Houk**, 26 years old and eight months pregnant, was found dead in her bed by the youngest of her two daughters, Adalynne, 4 years old. She was shot in the back of the head while she was sleeping. She died from the wound, and the baby, a boy who she had planned to name Christopher Allen, died from a lack of oxygen.

Kenzie had recently moved to a farmhouse in Wampum, Pennsylvania, with her daughters, her fiancé Christopher Brown and his 11-year-old son Jordan, who became the only suspect for her murder.

Police learned that Christopher left for work around 7 am, Kenzie was shot around 8 am and her body was found at 9.30 am. They interviewed Jordan and Kenzie's eldest daughter Jenessa, 7 years old, who were at home at the time of the murder. The boy told the investigators there was a black truck on the property that morning, sending them to follow a false lead for about five hours. His conflicting descriptions of the truck pushed them to reinterview Jenessa, who told them that on that morning Jordan had a shotgun covered in a blanket and that she heard a "big boom" before leaving for school with him. Afterwards, she saw him tossing something in the snow next to their driveway on their way to the school bus stop.

Sure enough, police found a youth-model 20-gauge shotgun, which Christopher had given to Jordan as a Christmas gift, outside the boy's bedroom, along with a blue blanket with a hole the size of a quarter and burn marks. Also, a shotgun shell was found near the path that Jenessa had described.

Based on her testimony and on the findings that validated it, police arrested Jordan Brown and, because of his age, kept him in isolation in the Lawrence County Jail.

The District Attorney John Bonivengo decided to prosecute Jordan as an adult, since the crime, in his opinion, was premeditated. He believed that the boy was jealous of Kenzie and having trouble adjusting to their blended family when she and her daughters moved in with him and his father. Kenzie's family accused Jordan of threating her and the girls at least two months before the killing. Her sister, Jennifer Kraner, stated: "We tried to love him. But there was some sort of issue". He also was a good shot, and won a turkey shoot less than two weeks earlier, beating out several adults. Jordan and his family refused to acknowledge his guilt.

In Pennsylvania, anyone 10 or older charged with homicide automatically starts in adult court. Defense attorneys can petition to move such cases to juvenile court, which Jordan's attorney Dennis Elisco did. Since the Lawrence County judge Dominick Motto found no evidence connecting anyone else to the killings, he initially rejected the petition. But after Pennsylvania Superior Court ruled that Judge Motto violated Jordan's Fifth Amendment, he reversed his earlier decision and, in August 2011, ruled that the boy should be tried as a juvenile.

Lawrence County family court judge John Hodge issued his ruling on April 13, 2012, that Jordan was responsible for first-degree murder, adjudicated him to be delinquent (the juvenile court equivalent of a guilty verdict) and ordered him to a juvenile facility.

His attorney said that Jordan, now 19, is doing well, he completed all programs and met all juvenile rehabilitation goals and is in no further need of detention. Indeed, he was released from juvenile custody on June 2016. He is now free, even if technically on juvenile probation until he turns 21.

6- Amarjeet Sada

Amarjeet (or Amardeep) Sada made himself known as a gruesome young killer not only in his own country, India, but all over the world as "India's youngest serial killer".

In January 2007, Chunchun Devi, a young mother residing in Musahri, Bihar, India, left her six-month-old daughter Khushboo to sleep at the village primary school while she attended to household chores. When she returned, she found that the baby had disappeared.

The Musahri villagers immediately confronted an 8-year-old boy, Amarjeet Sada, son of an impoverished Indian couple of the neighbourhood, who happily confessed that he had strangled Khushboo and hit her with a brick before attempting to bury the body in the nearby field, covering it with grass and leaves. He even led them to the spot. They turned him over to authorities on May 30, 2007, and his parents fled the village before police came.

The residents started calling Amarjeet a "mini" serial-killer, admitting that they were extra careful around him because during the previous year he had allegedly killed his sister and cousin too, both around the same age as Khushboo, with the same *modus operandi*. However, there is no official confirmation of these two killings, they had never been reported, since they were considered a "family matter".

When he was arrested and questioned, Amarjeet allegedly said to police: "Khapda se mar mar ke suta deliyay (I killed by beating her with a brick)". Inspector Shatrudhan Kumar of Bihar police stated that the boy spoke little but smiled a lot, asking for biscuits.

Experts who examined the boy said that he appeared to be a sadist who derived pleasure from inflicting injuries and that he didn't have a sense of right or wrong.

Not much more has ever been released about this case, just that Amarjeet was charged with murder for Khushboo's death and tried as a juvenile. But, since in the Indian law the maximum punishment for juvenile is three years, it's possible that he served the rest of his sentence in a psychiatric institute.

Also, rumor has it that he changed his name to "Samarjit" and managed to recover from his conduct disorder through rehabilitation and treatment.

7- Jesse Pomeroy

Dubbed the "Boy Fiend" by the press, Jesse Harding Pomeroy stood out for not only having been one of the youngest serial killers ever known, but also the youngest person convicted for first-degree murder in the history of Massachusetts.

South Boston, Massachusetts, April 21, 1874. 4-year-old **Horace Millen**, dark brown eyes and shiny blonde locks of hair, convinced his mother to let him go to the local bakery to buy some sweets, which he loved. Mrs Millen dressed him fancily, gave him a couple of pennies and that was the last time she saw him alive. She and her husband John had been searching for him for hours before they decided to report his missing to police that very evening. Little did they know that Horace's corpse was already being exanimated by the coroner.

At 4 pm that day, two brothers were playing along the beach at Dorchester Bay, near Boston, and spotted what looked like a rag doll at the bottom of the small valley. It was Horace. The little boy had been tortured and viciously slashed with a knife to his death. He was nearly decapitated because of numerous stabs to the neck, it appeared that he had tried to defend himself, as his body showed dozen defense wounds, but he also had to suffer 18 stabs to the torso, an eyeball being punctured and the mutilation of his genitals. He had died an excruciating death, as his tightly clenched fists proved. Whoever did this was a monster.

The body was unidentified at first and the police issued a bulletin to all stations for help in identifying him and shortly after 9 pm a police officer of the South Boston precinct was dispatched to the Millen home in Dorchester Street with awful news.

There was only a suspect: Jesse Pomeroy.

The first 14 years of his life (1859-1874) were made of violence. Not much is known about his early childhood, besides that he was the second son of a lower middle class family in the Chelsea section of Boston, and that his father used to savagely beat him. He looked different from other children, mostly because of the cataract in his right eye, that was almost pure white, giving him an evil aura. Like many future killers, Jesse enjoyed torturing animals, but soon grew weary of it and in winter 1871 began to look for human targets.

At least seven boys, aged 4 to 8, had been lured to secluded places to be severely beaten, tortured and, in some cases, nearly killed by someone they could only describe only as "a teenage boy with brown hair". In spite of a massive manhunt by police, the "inhuman scamp", as the papers called the unknown pervert, managed to spread fear in the Chelsea and South Boston areas between 1871 and 1872.

The last victim, 5-year-old Robert Gould, gave police their first good lead in the case, describing his attacker as a "large boy with an eye like a white marble". On September 21, 1872, police brought one of the other victims, 7-year- old Joseph Kennedy, to a classroom-by-classroom search in Jesse Pomeroy's school and they arrested him hours later just outside the South Boston police station, after he inexplicably showed up there and was recognized by Joseph.

Being the sociopath he was, he did it because he probably felt powerless to stop himself and wanted to be caught.

Upon questioning he claimed his innocence, but police insisted on trying to force him to confess his crimes, which he eventually did. He was brought before a magistrate, to whom he said "I couldn't help myself" and was ordered to be held in the House of Reformation in Westborough, Massachusetts, until he was 18.

Jesse learned very quickly that his only chance to leave Westborough as soon as possible was to demonstrate that he had reformed his ways, so he became a model inmate and was released in early 1874, less than a year-and-a-half after his arrest. None of the authorities thought of warning his neighbours.

When Horace Millen was killed and police learned that Jesse Pomeroy had been paroled, he became their prime suspect. They took him from home and interrogated him. Despite the fact that he was unable to offer up an alibi, had fresh scratch marks on his face, marsh grass stuck to his shoes, a bloodstain on his undershirt and a three-inch blade knife with dried blood on the handle, he continued to deny involvement. Until they showed him Horace's corpse. He broke down and admitted to the murder.

Jesse had encountered Horace on the way to the bakery shop and convinced him to spend some time together. The little boy bought a small cake and shared it with Jesse before the two of them headed to the nearby harbour. A number of witnesses saw the pair but none suspected what was about to happen. Jesse took Horace to a deserted area and they stopped in a swale. The moment Horace sat down, the other took out his pocket knife and slashed the little boy's throat. He hacked him repeatedly on all his body to his death, especially in the genital area, attempting to castrate him.

But it soon turned out that Horace Millen was not the only child Jesse Pomeroy had killed.

His mother, Ruth Pomeroy, ran a dressmaking shop and Jesse, his elder brother Charles and a young employee by the name of Rudolph Kohr, helped her. Before the trial for Horace Millen's even began, Ruth had to shut down the shop, which was taken by another tenant. Upon refurbishing the basement of the former Pomeroys' shop, the workmen found the beheaded and rotting body of 10-year-old Katie Mary Curran, who had been missing for a month.

Jesse tried to deny this crime too, but confessed when police convinced him that they could have accused his mother and brother instead.

On the morning of March 18, 1874, Jesse and Rudolph were opening up the shop when Katie came in, asking for a notebook she needed before going to school. Jesse sent Rudolph out for a commission, lured Katie to the basement with him saying they would find a notebook for her and he reportedly "followed her, put [his] arm around her neck, [his] hand over her mouth, **and with [his] knife cut her throat**". He then proceeded with brutally attacking her abdomen and genitals, hiding her body in the water closet, washing his hands and going back to work as if nothing happened.

The trial opened on December 8, 1874. Prosecutor John May presented substantial evidence against Jesse, also calling witnesses, from the police officers who investigated Horace's murder to the jail minister who heard his confession. His argument was also supported by one of the three specialists of mental disorders that had examined Jesse. Dr. George T. Choate contradicted the two defense doctors, who considered Jesse insane, calling him "cunning and deeply manipulative" and concluding that he was free of mental defect.

Jesse's lawyer, Charles Robinson, tried to have him declared a legally insane, which could have saved him from the gallows and committed him to a lunatic hospital. He stated before the jury that Jesse was unable to control his impulses, so he wasn't to blame. Calling as witnesses the victims of Jesse's molestation to show how much crazy he was only managed to convince the jury to never acquit Jesse.

The next day, the jury found Jesse Pomeroy guilty of first-degree murder, for which the mandatory sentence by the law of Massachusetts was death by hanging.

Such a sentence was only within the power of the governor to grant, but Governor William Gaston didn't want to take this decision for political reasons. In August 1876, the new governor, Alexander Rice, granting the jury's recommendation of mercy on account of Jesse's young age, decided to commute his death sentence to life in prison, to serve in solitary confinement.

On September 7, 1876, Jesse was incarcerated at the Charlestown State Prison, where he remained in solitary confinement for 40 years, that he spent studying foreign languages and law and trying to escape numerous times. In 1917, his sentence of solitary confinement was relaxed and he was allowed to move to the general population, until his health began to deteriorate.

Aged 71, in 1929, Jesse Pomeroy was removed from Charlestown State Prison and had his first and last automobile ride to Bridgewater prison farm, where he died two years later, never showing any remorse or pity for his victims.

8- Eric Smith

A loner and bullied boy who, overwhelmed by pain and anger, killed a 4-year-old is still seen as a symbol of the loss of innocence. Eric Smith is guilty of one of the most horrific crimes committed by a child in modern times.

Soon to be 5-year-old **Derrick Robie** was known as the unofficial mayor of the tiny village of Savona, New York, because he used to sit on his bike and wave to cars that went by the streets. In the morning of August 2, 1993, he was ready to go to his summer recreation program, that was being held in a park only a block away from his home. His mother Doreen couldn't walk him, as she usually did, because she had to take care of her youngest son Dalton, who was just a baby at the time. Derrick insisted he could go on his own, he kissed his mother, said that he loved her, and off he went.

Around 11 am, Doreen went to the park to pick him up and found out that Derrick had never arrived there.

His body was found hours later in a small patch of woods, halfway between the park where he was headed and his home. Evidence found that the killer had lured Derrick from the sidewalk and strangled him. He then had dug up a very large rock and a smaller one and battered the boy with them. But this was not enough for him. He had smashed a banana that Derrick had in his lunch bag and also taken a Kool Aid to pour it in the wounds in the head. He had concluded with sodomizing the poor child with a small stick and posed the body in a specific position, removing the shoes and arranging them around it. The cause of death was determined to be blunt trauma to the head with contributing asphyxia.

Initially, these disturbing details of the crime were not made public, but some years later the Robie family insisted that the whole story had to be told, in order to prevent Derrick's killer to be set free.

Four days later, 13-year-old Eric Smith walked into the police command center to see if he could be of help in solving the crime. He repeatedly talked to investigator John Hibsch, to whom he denied seeing Derrick the day he was murdered. Only to abruptly change the story shortly after, almost knocking Hibsch off the chair saying "Right across the street from the open field. And that's when I saw Derrick", putting himself right on top of the crime scene. He consequently was able to describe the boy's clothing and the fact that he had a lunch bag in his hand before he started getting emotional, also by throwing on the ground a glass of Kool Aid his father had brought him.

Eric M. Smith, red hair, freckles and thick glasses, was a troubled boy, born with development delays caused by an epilepsy drug his mother Tammy had taken during pregnancy, and relentlessly bullied by older children at school. As a toddler, he threw temper tantrums and banged his head on the floor and growing up his anger issues had worsened, so much that he had asked for help to his stepfather, Ted. On the other hand, he enjoyed spending time with his grandparents, Red and Edie Wilson, that he would always hug and kiss.

When some details about the murder were released in the local news, Eric's family and neighbours started suspecting his involvement, also remembering how much Eric hated bananas. To the point that he could have had a reason to smash the banana of Derrick's lunch bag in a burst of anger.

All of them knew that Eric was hiding something, but "in no way did we [felt] he had done it" and begged him to tell what he knew.

All evidence was against young Eric and it took him three more days to confess to the murder, a couple of days after Derrick's funeral.

The trial took place in August 1994 and it was focused on giving an answer to the question "Why did Eric kill?".

Eric's defense attorney Kevin Bradley, with the testimony of psychiatrist Dr. Stephen Herman, pointed out that the boy suffered from a very serious mental disease, an intermittent explosive disorder causing individuals to act out violently and unpredictably. In conclusion, Eric didn't know he was doing something wrong, his pain and rage just overwhelmed him. Quoting Bradley: "The fact that he seemed normal afterwards shows he is not normal".

Instead, the prosecution believed that Eric indeed knew full well that his actions were wrong because he admitted that he had lured Derrick into the woods for the killing so no one could see. Prosecutor John Tunney concluded that Eric chose to do something horrible on purpose. "He can have every psychological, psychiatric problem in the world, and he's still responsible for what he did, under the law" he stated.

Because of the sexual nature of the crime, the question of whether Eric was abused was repeatedly raised at trial, but there was no evidence that anyone had sexually abused him and he himself denied it years later.

Throughout his trial, the boy showed no emotion, expressed no remorse and never explained why he killed Derrick.

On August 14, 1994, the jury unanimously found him guilty of murder in the second degree and he was consequently sentenced to the maximum sentence for a juvenile: nine years to life in prison.

Eric was held at Brookwood Juvenile Detention Center and then transferred to the maximum security adult prison Clinton Correctional Facility in Dannemora, New York, when he turned 21 in 2001. He is currently incarcerated at medium security prison for male inmates Collins Correctional Facility in Erie County, New York.

He has been denied parole eight times since 2002. During his last parole board in April 2016, his new attorney Susan Betzjitomir, who believes that he should be released, allowed him to read a statement he prepared to demonstrate that he has changed. He apologized to Derrick and his family and gave a chilling explanation for the killing: "Because instead of me being hurt, I was hurting someone else."

Even this time, Parole Board found that Eric's release would pose a risk to "the public safety and welfare of the community".

He will next be eligible for parole in April 2018.

To honor Derrick, volunteers bulldozed the scene of the crime and put in a new ball field in memory of the little T-ball player. The Robie family still lives in Savona and has not exchanged a single word with the Smith's since Derrick's murder.

9- Christopher Pittman

Because of its controversy both in the American legal and medical system, his case was faced by courts and media like the Jordan

Brown's case, but, unlike Jordan, Christopher Pittman was persecuted as an adult.

Married couple **Joe, 66 years old, and Joy Pittman, 62 years old**, residing in Chester, South Carolina, were shot to death in their bed during the night of November 28, 2001, and their house was set on fire.

The next day, two counties away, police caught the Pittmans' 12-year-old grandson, Christopher, driving their car. He also had with him their dog, their guns and $ 33, all stolen from them. He told a story of a large black male who had kidnapped him after killing his grandparents and setting fire to the house, but he eventually confessed to the murder, proclaiming that "they deserved what they got".

Christopher Frank Pittman was depressed because he felt abandoned by his mother and the relationship with his father, Joe, was troubled. He suffered to the point that he ran away from their home in Florida and threatened to kill himself. He was hospitalized in a facility for troubled children, where he was diagnosed with mild chronic depression accompanied by defiant and negative behaviour and put on Paxil, an antidepressant. But his father decided to remove him from there six days later and to send him to live with his paternal grandparents in South Carolina, where a doctor, having no samples of Paxil to give, prescribed him another antidepressant, Zoloft.

Maybe suffering from too high a dose of Zoloft or from Paxil withdrawal, Christopher allegedly began to experience negative side-effects from the new medication almost immediately, even if there is also evidence that issues began before he even went on Paxil.

After a few weeks in Chester, the boy got into a dispute on a school bus, where he chocked another student, and behaved unruly during a church service. His grandparents disciplined him, threatening to send him back to his father. That same night, he waited for the old couple to go to sleep, stole his grandfather's shotgun from a cabinet and killed them as they slept in their beds. Then, he set the house on fire and fled.

Since South Carolina sets no minimum age for trying defendants as adults, Christopher was convicted in adult court, despite the efforts of his defense lawyer Arnold "Andy" Vickery to get the case heard in family court.

His trial began on January 31, 2005, three years after the murders.

While the prosecution countered that Christopher simply killed his grandparents out of anger towards them, pointing his statement to police in which he, lucid and clear, said that they deserved it, the defense claimed that the boy was involuntarily intoxicated by Zoloft and lost control, hence he committed manslaughter, not murder.

The forensic psychiatric who examined Christopher for prosecution, Dr. Pamela M. Crawford, concluded in her report that the boy knew what he was doing because he provided "nonpsychotic reasons" for killing his grandparents, tried to cover up the crime, fled and made self-protective statements to avoid arrest.

Christopher stated that his mood changed on the Zoloft medication, to the extent that he "didn't have any feelings". He was allegedly hearing voices telling him to commit the crime and, in a letter that was read on court by his father, he wrote: "Through the whole thing, it was like watching your favourite TV show. You know what is going to happen but you can't do anything to stop it".

The trial was focused on the debate about the real effects the antidepressant, made by Pfizer Inc., has on children and teens. Studies showed reports linked to suicidal behaviour, not homicidal, so medical experts didn't believe there was a link between antidepressant and acts of extreme violence. Only a handful of psychiatrists have ever argued that the negative side-effects can unleash rages so uncontrollable as to overwhelm a person's ability to distinguish between right and wrong and commit murder.

On February 15, 2005, Christopher Pittman was found guilty of first-degree murder, as required by prosecution, and sentenced to 30 years in prison, which was the minimum penalty the judge could give. The maximum sentence was life in prison.

If he had been convicted in family court as a juvenile, he could have been kept in custody only until he turned 21.

In December 2010, aged 21, Christopher pleaded guilty to two counts of voluntary manslaughter and his sentence was reduced to 25 years.

He's not eligible for parole and will "max out" his sentence in 2023.

Now he's a 28-year-old model inmate and his family, especially his older sister Danielle Pittman Finchum and his maternal grandmother Delnora Duprey, strongly believe in his innocence, claiming that Christopher was pushed to kill by his prescribed drugs. They often go and visit him in his prison in Allendale, South Carolina.

10- Lionel Tate

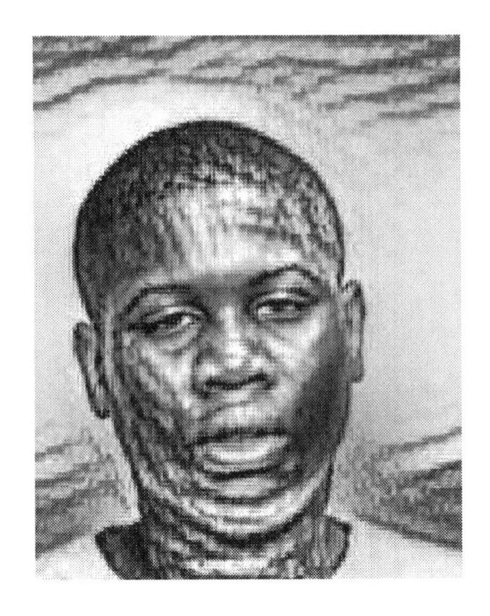

Despite being the youngest American citizen ever sentenced to life imprisonment without possibility of parole, Lionel Alexander Tate has had many chances to change his fate but chose to live a life full of "mistakes" instead.

On July 28, 1999, Florida Highway Patrol trooper Kathleen Grosset-Tate was babysitting 6-year-old **Tiffany Eunick** at her home in Miramar. She left her alone playing with her son Lionel, aged 12, who had a reputation as a schoolyard bully.

The boy decided to demonstrate with the little girl some pro-wrestling techniques that he enjoyed seeing on the "WWF Smackdown" tv show. He punched, threw and kicked her to death.

Lionel, who weighed 170 pounds at the time, stomped on her so forcefully that her liver was lacerated and part of it broke loose and was floating free inside her body. Also, part of her brain flattened inside her head, her skull was fractured and her ribs were cracked. These injuries were later described as "similar to those she would have sustained by falling from a three-story building".

He then just went to his mother saying that Tiffany was not breathing.

When police came to arrest him, Lionel claimed to have accidentally thrown her into the banister of the stairs instead of onto the couch. Upon further pressure from police, he told the whole story.

Kathleen fiercely defended his son claiming that Tiffany's death was just a tragic accident, both she and the defense attorney Jim Lewis were certain of Lionel's acquittal, to the extent that they even rejected a plea bargain agreement offered by prosecution that would have had the boy serving only three years of jail time in a juvenile center, one year of house arrest plus ten years of probation on a second-degree charge.

So, Lionel was put on trial as an adult. His case went before Judge Joel T. Lazarus of Broward County Circuit Court in Fort Lauderdale, Florida.

Jim Lewis's defense was based upon the boy's love of professional wrestling, blaming the acts of extreme violence depicted by the World Wrestling Federation for Tiffany's death. In essence, Lionel should have been pitied and not punished.

But there was plenty of evidence suggesting his guilt. As prosecutor Ken Padowitz argued, Lionel knew that his actions were wrong, which, as per the so-called "felony murder rule", was enough to have him convicted for first-degree murder. "He didn't say 'I'm going to kill Tiffany Eunick'", he said. "All that is required is that he intended to act, not that he intended the result".

In January 2001, after three hours of deliberation, the jury returned in courtroom with a guilty verdict.

Judge Lazarus, believing that Lionel's guilt was "clear, obvious and indisputable" handed down Florida's mandatory sentence for defendants convicted of first-degree murder: life in prison without parole. He said: "The acts of Lionel Tate were not the playful acts of a child [...] The acts of Lionel Tate were cold, callous and indescribably cruel".

The sentence was controversial due to both Lionel's and Tiffany's young age, bringing broad criticism on the treatment of juvenile offenders in the justice system of the State of Florida, applying the felony murder rule without having to prove that Lionel intended any harm.

In January 2004, a state appeals court overturned Lionel's conviction on the basis that his mental competency had not been evaluated before trial. This led the young man, 17-years-old at the time, to plea guilty of second-degree murder in exchange for one year's house arrest followed by ten years' probation, the same agreement his mother had originally turned down.

Lionel was released, only to be apprehended and held in prison eight months later for violating the terms of his house arrest. He was found by police a few blocks away from his house in the middle of the night carrying an eight-inch knife.

When released again, he was allowed to return to Kathleen Grossett-Tate's home.

On May 23, 2005, Lionel was charged with armed burglary with battery, armed robbery and violation of probation for his involvement in the assault of a Domino's Pizza deliveryman by the name of Walter Ernest Gallardo. He admitted his guilt but refused to answer questions about where he got and later disposed of the gun used to threaten Gallardo, which was never recovered.

He was finally sentenced to 30 years in prison on May 18, 2006.**3**

Lionel Tate is currently being held at Everglades Correction Institution in Miami-Dade County, Florida, and is scheduled to be released on September 16, 2030.

About Lionel's case, for which he was the prosecutor, Ken Padowitz recently stated that it "did have an impact on [American] legislation", helping in providing "alternatives that are appropriate age-based punishments and rehabilitation".

Published by VAX Books

VaxbookZ.com

Printed in Great Britain
by Amazon

50862835R00040